LOCKDOWN: VOLUME 2

It is a time of uncertainty in the galaxy. Standing against the oppression of the First Order is the Resistance, including Poe Dameron and his team of ace pilots — Black Squadron.

General Leia Organa has tasked Poe to locate information vital to the survival of the Resistance. Their first mission has revealed a new enemy: Agent Terex of the First Order Security Bureau. Though Black Squadron has survived the encounter, Terex has vowed to destroy them.

Now, Poe and his team have arrived at Megalox Beta, a prison complex secured by the extremely high gravity of the planet's surface. The prison has no walls or guards. The prisoners make the rules, and all answer to Grakkus the Hutt....

CHARLES SOULE
Writer

PHIL NOTO
Artist

VC's JOE CARAMAGNA
Letterer

PHIL NOTO
Cover Artist

HEATHER ANTOS
Assistant Editor

JORDAN D. WHITE
Editor

C.B. CEBULSKI
Executive Editor

AXEL ALONSO
Editor In Chief

JOE QUESADA
Chief Creative Officer

DAN BUCKLEY
Publisher

For Lucasfilm:
Senior Editor FRANK PARISI
Creative Director MICHAEL SIGLAIN
Lucasfilm Story Group RAYNE ROBERTS, PABLO HIDALGO, LELAND CHEE, MATT MARTIN

ABDO
Spotlight

ABDOPUBLISHING.COM

Reinforced library bound edition published in 2018 by Spotlight,
a division of ABDO, PO Box 398166, Minneapolis, Minnesota 55439.
Spotlight produces high-quality reinforced library bound editions for
schools and libraries. Published by agreement with Marvel Characters, Inc.

Printed in the United States of America, North Mankato, Minnesota.
092017
012018

 THIS BOOK CONTAINS
RECYCLED MATERIALS

marvelkids.com

STAR WARS © & TM 2018 LUCASFILM LTD.

PUBLISHER'S CATALOGING-IN-PUBLICATION DATA

Names: Soule, Charles, author. | Noto, Phil, illustrator.
Title: Lockdown / writer: Charles Soule ; art: Phil Noto.
Description: Minneapolis, MN : Spotlight, 2018 | Series: Star Wars: Poe Dameron
Summary: After escaping Agent Terex and the First Order, Poe and the Black
    Squadron find themselves at prison complex Megalox Beta to talk with prisoner
    Grakkus the Hutt, but a vengeful enemy has beaten the squad there, and
    Grakkus will only give his information to the team that breaks him out of jail
    first.
Identifiers: LCCN 2017941921 | ISBN 9781532141379 (v.1 ; lib. bdg.) | ISBN
    9781532141386 (v.2 ; lib. bdg.) | ISBN 9781532141393 (v.3 ; lib. bdg.)
Subjects: LCSH: Star Wars (film)--Juvenile fiction. | Adventure and Adventurers--
    Juvenile fiction. | Graphic Novels--Juvenile fiction.
Classification: DDC 741.5--dc23
LC record available at http://lccn.loc.gov/2017941921

Spotlight

A Division of ABDO
abdopublishing.com

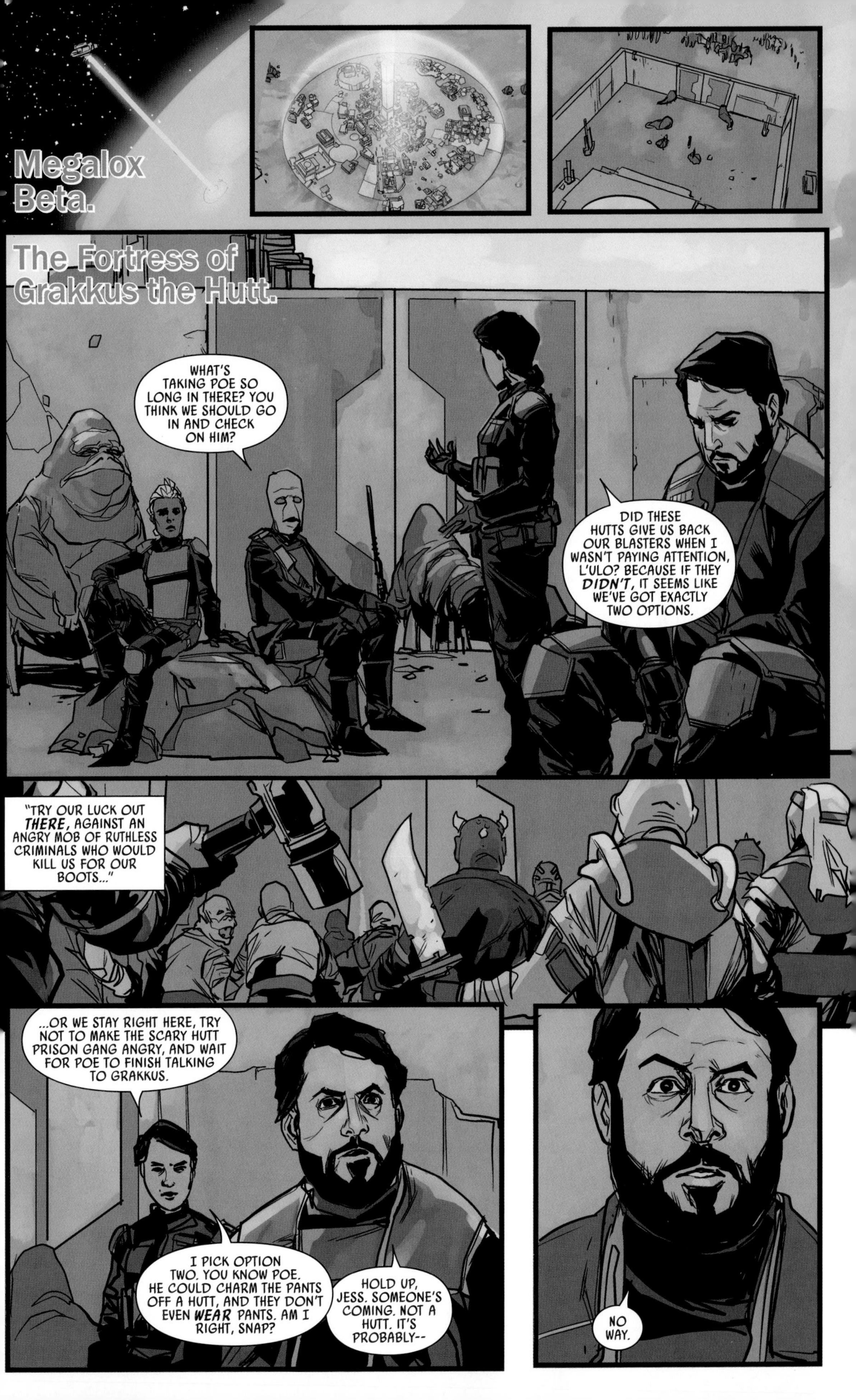
Megalox Beta.
The Fortress of Grakkus the Hutt.
WHAT'S TAKING POE SO LONG IN THERE? YOU THINK WE SHOULD GO IN AND CHECK ON HIM?
DID THESE HUTTS GIVE US BACK OUR BLASTERS WHEN I WASN'T PAYING ATTENTION, L'ULO? BECAUSE IF THEY DIDN'T, IT SEEMS LIKE WE'VE GOT EXACTLY TWO OPTIONS.
"TRY OUR LUCK OUT THERE, AGAINST AN ANGRY MOB OF RUTHLESS CRIMINALS WHO WOULD KILL US FOR OUR BOOTS..."
...OR WE STAY RIGHT HERE, TRY NOT TO MAKE THE SCARY HUTT PRISON GANG ANGRY, AND WAIT FOR POE TO FINISH TALKING TO GRAKKUS.
I PICK OPTION TWO. YOU KNOW POE. HE COULD CHARM THE PANTS OFF A HUTT, AND THEY DON'T EVEN WEAR PANTS. AM I RIGHT, SNAP?
HOLD UP, JESS. SOMEONE'S COMING. NOT A HUTT. IT'S PROBABLY--
NO WAY.

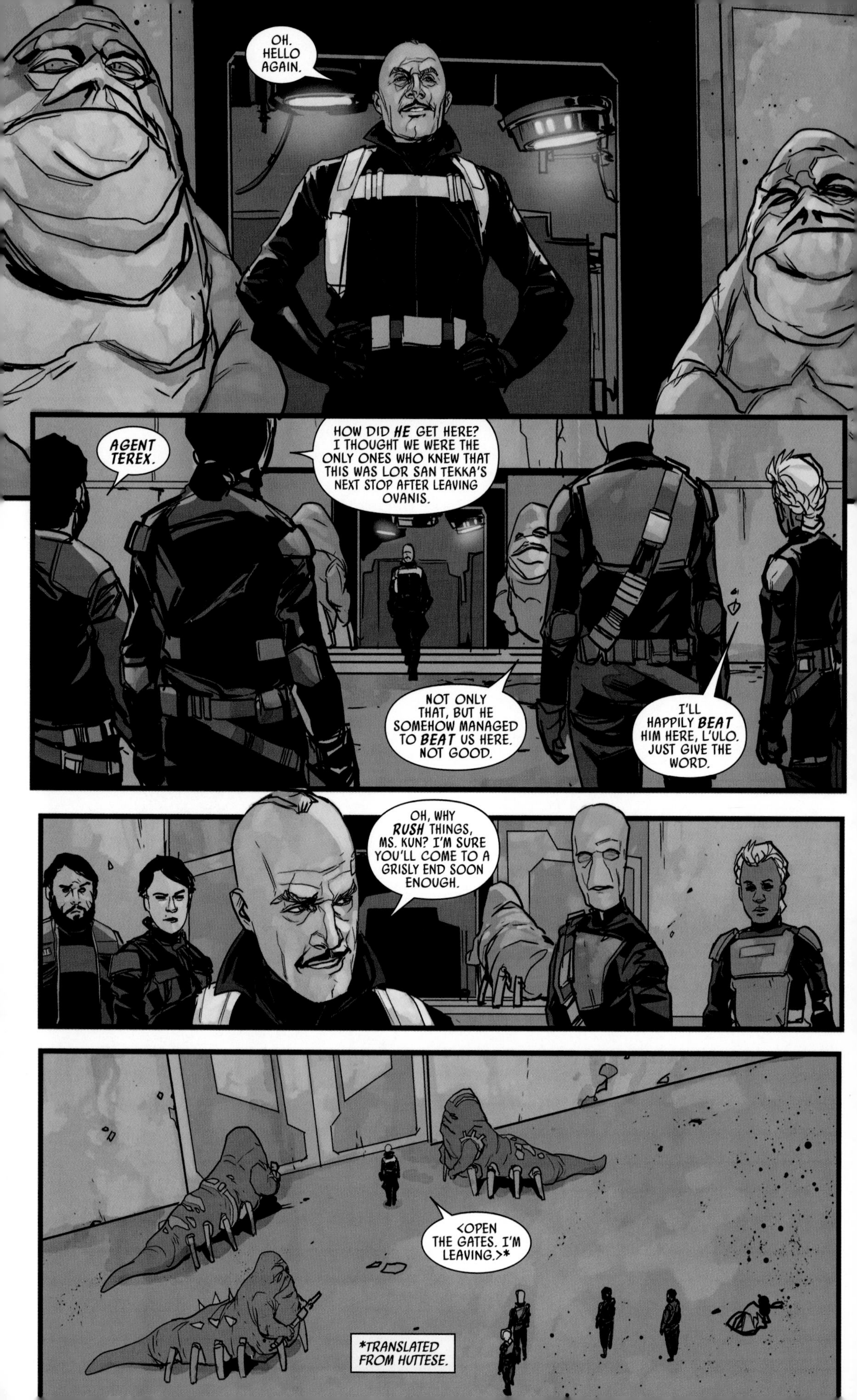
OH. HELLO AGAIN.
AGENT TEREX.
HOW DID HE GET HERE? I THOUGHT WE WERE THE ONLY ONES WHO KNEW THAT THIS WAS LOR SAN TEKKA'S NEXT STOP AFTER LEAVING OVANIS.
NOT ONLY THAT, BUT HE SOMEHOW MANAGED TO BEAT US HERE. NOT GOOD.
I'LL HAPPILY BEAT HIM HERE, L'ULO. JUST GIVE THE WORD.
OH, WHY RUSH THINGS, MS. KUN? I'M SURE YOU'LL COME TO A GRISLY END SOON ENOUGH.
<OPEN THE GATES. I'M LEAVING.>*
*TRANSLATED FROM HUTTESE.

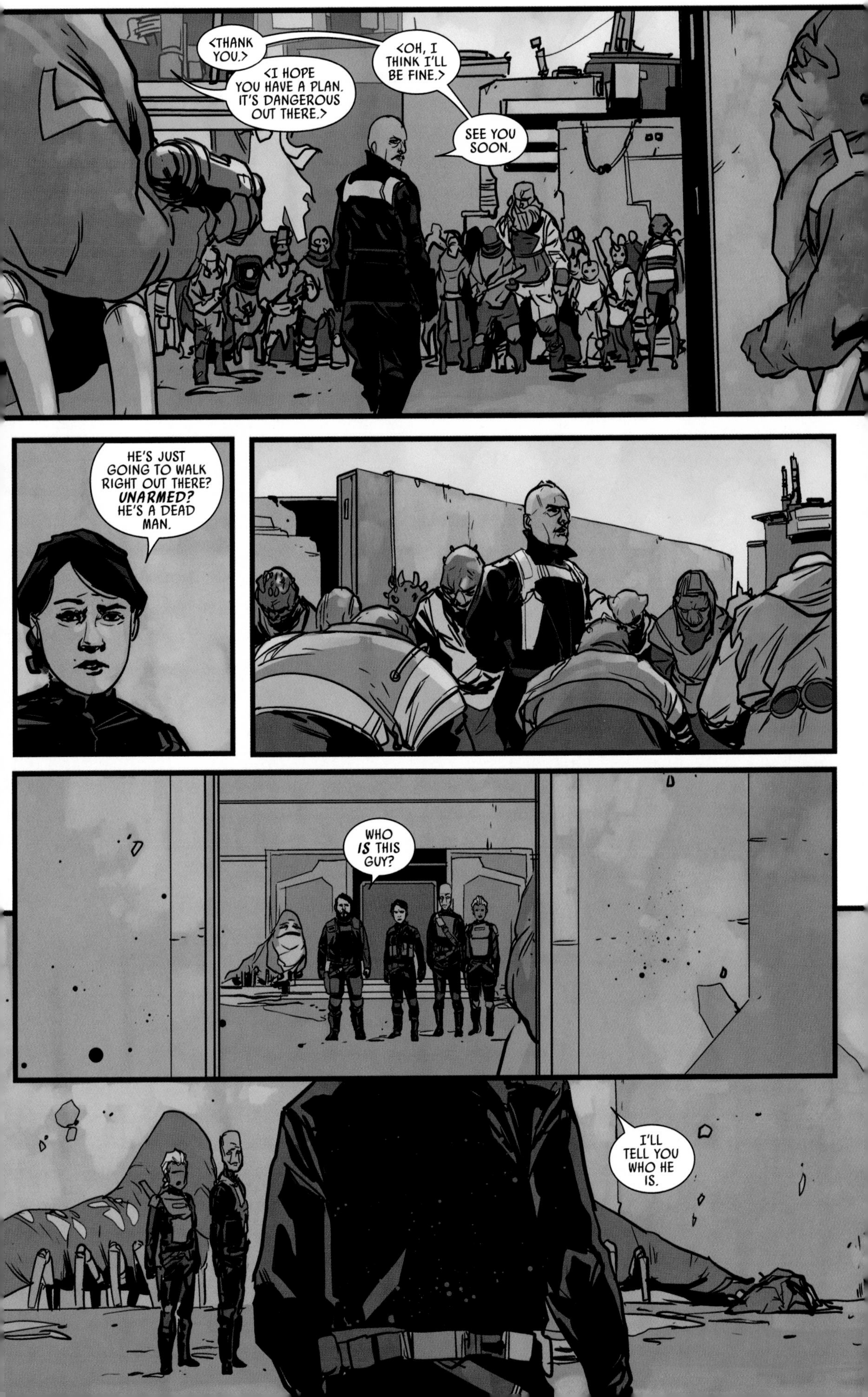

<THANK YOU.>
<I HOPE YOU HAVE A PLAN. IT'S DANGEROUS OUT THERE.>
<OH, I THINK I'LL BE FINE.>
SEE YOU SOON.
HE'S JUST GOING TO WALK RIGHT OUT THERE? UNARMED? HE'S A DEAD MAN.
WHO IS THIS GUY?
I'LL TELL YOU WHO HE IS.

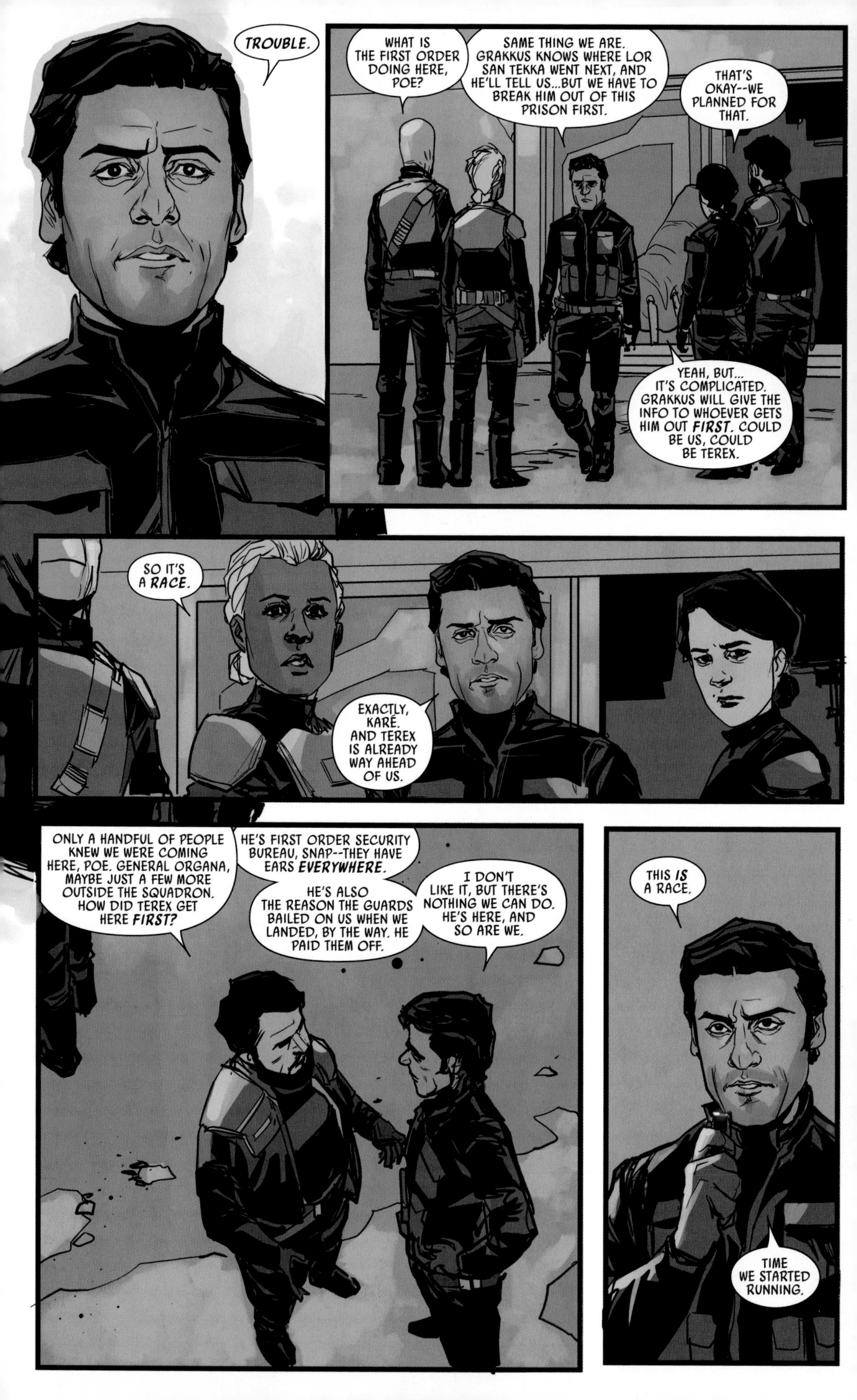
TROUBLE.
WHAT IS THE FIRST ORDER DOING HERE, POE?
SAME THING WE ARE. GRAKKUS KNOWS WHERE LOR SAN TEKKA WENT NEXT, AND HE'LL TELL US...BUT WE HAVE TO BREAK HIM OUT OF THIS PRISON FIRST.
THAT'S OKAY--WE PLANNED FOR THAT.
YEAH, BUT... IT'S COMPLICATED. GRAKKUS WILL GIVE THE INFO TO WHOEVER GETS HIM OUT FIRST. COULD BE US, COULD BE TEREX.
SO IT'S A RACE.
EXACTLY, KARÉ. AND TEREX IS ALREADY WAY AHEAD OF US.
ONLY A HANDFUL OF PEOPLE KNEW WE WERE COMING HERE, POE. GENERAL ORGANA, MAYBE JUST A FEW MORE OUTSIDE THE SQUADRON. HOW DID TEREX GET HERE FIRST?
HE'S FIRST ORDER SECURITY BUREAU, SNAP--THEY HAVE EARS EVERYWHERE.
HE'S ALSO THE REASON THE GUARDS BAILED ON US WHEN WE LANDED, BY THE WAY. HE PAID THEM OFF.
I DON'T LIKE IT, BUT THERE'S NOTHING WE CAN DO. HE'S HERE, AND SO ARE WE.
THIS IS A RACE.
TIME WE STARTED RUNNING.

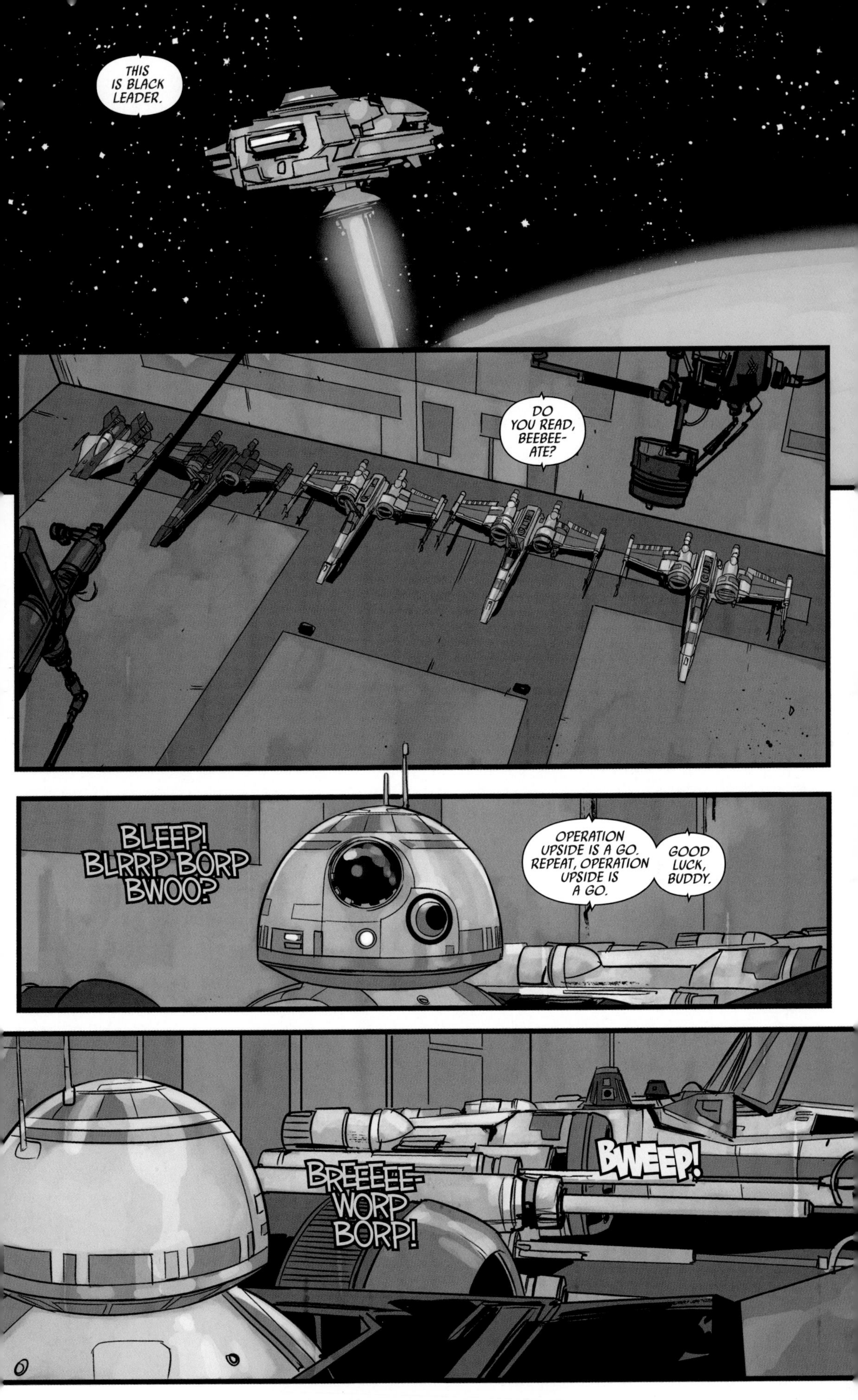

THIS IS BLACK LEADER.
DO YOU READ, BEEBEE-ATE?
BLEEP! BLRRP BORP BWOO?
OPERATION UPSIDE IS A GO. REPEAT, OPERATION UPSIDE IS A GO.
GOOD LUCK, BUDDY.
BREEEEE-WORP BORP!
BWEEP!

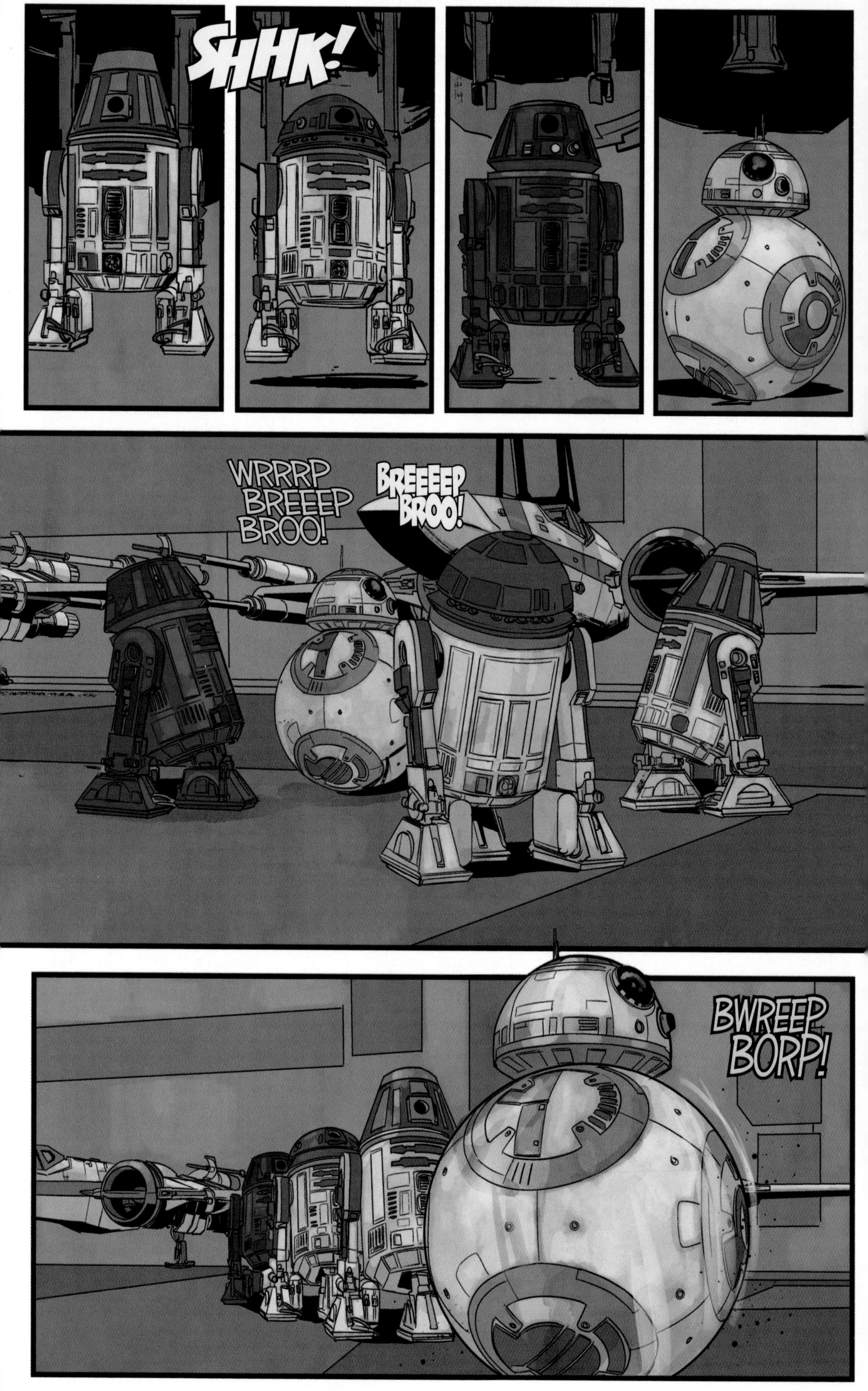
SHHK!
WRRRP BREEEP BROO!
BREEEEP BROO!
BWREEP BORP!

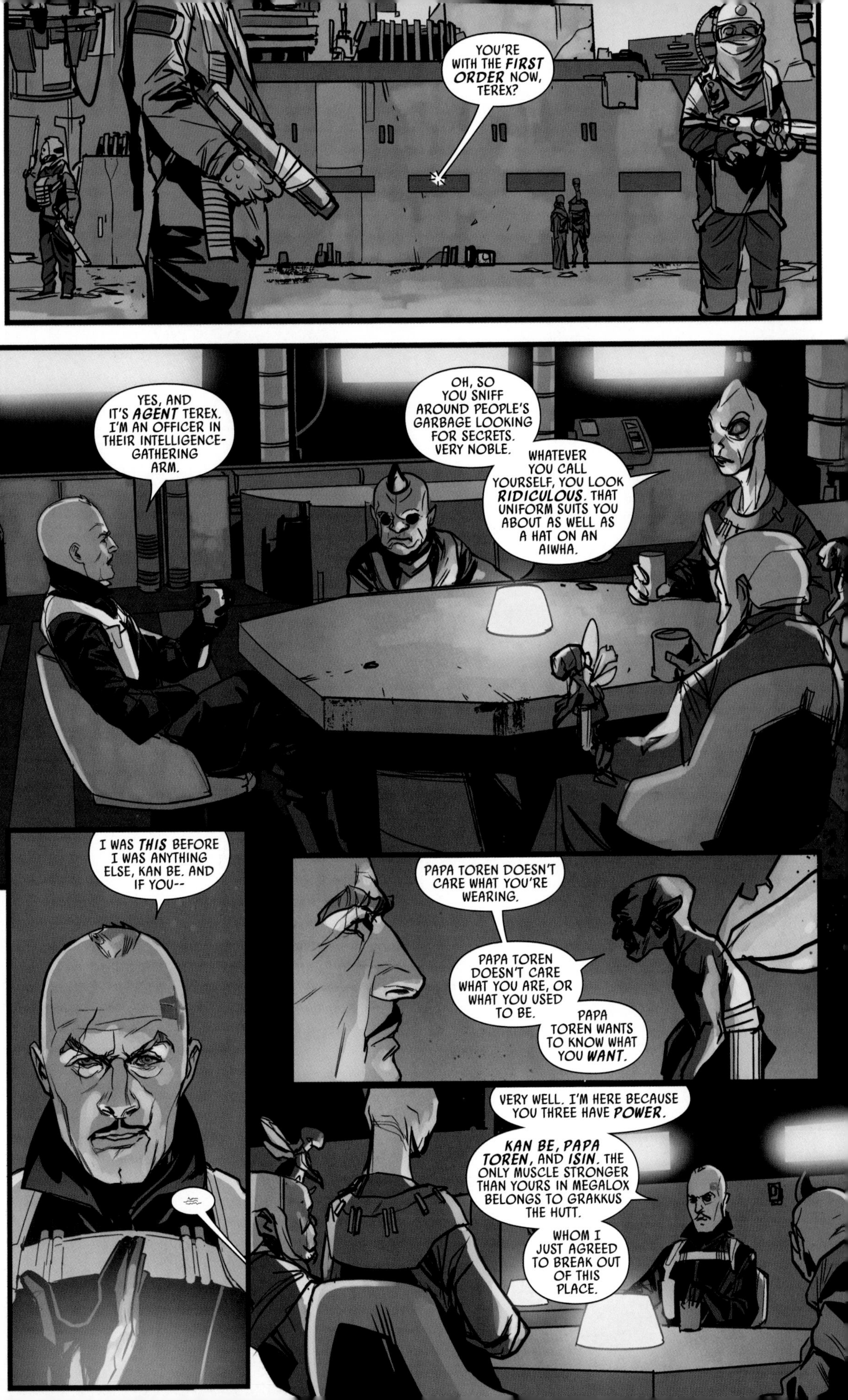

YOU'RE WITH THE FIRST ORDER NOW, TEREX?
YES, AND IT'S AGENT TEREX. I'M AN OFFICER IN THEIR INTELLIGENCE-GATHERING ARM.
OH, SO YOU SNIFF AROUND PEOPLE'S GARBAGE LOOKING FOR SECRETS. VERY NOBLE.
WHATEVER YOU CALL YOURSELF, YOU LOOK RIDICULOUS. THAT UNIFORM SUITS YOU ABOUT AS WELL AS A HAT ON AN AIWHA.
I WAS THIS BEFORE I WAS ANYTHING ELSE, KAN BE. AND IF YOU--
PAPA TOREN DOESN'T CARE WHAT YOU'RE WEARING.
PAPA TOREN DOESN'T CARE WHAT YOU ARE, OR WHAT YOU USED TO BE.
PAPA TOREN WANTS TO KNOW WHAT YOU WANT.
VERY WELL. I'M HERE BECAUSE YOU THREE HAVE POWER.
KAN BE, PAPA TOREN, AND ISIN. THE ONLY MUSCLE STRONGER THAN YOURS IN MEGALOX BELONGS TO GRAKKUS THE HUTT.
WHOM I JUST AGREED TO BREAK OUT OF THIS PLACE.

YOU'RE GOING TO GET GRAKKUS OUT? YOU REALLY THINK YOU SHOULD RUB THAT IN OUR FACES?

PAPA TOREN SAYS WE SHOULD CUT HIM UP AND DROP HIM IN THE STEWPOTS.

HE SAYS THERE'S NEVER ENOUGH FOOD DOWN HERE AS IT IS.

RELAX, ALL OF YOU.

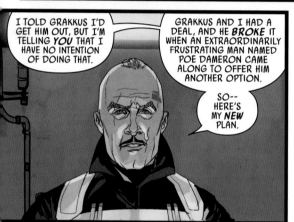

I TOLD GRAKKUS I'D GET HIM OUT, BUT I'M TELLING YOU THAT I HAVE NO INTENTION OF DOING THAT.

GRAKKUS AND I HAD A DEAL, AND HE BROKE IT WHEN AN EXTRAORDINARILY FRUSTRATING MAN NAMED POE DAMERON CAME ALONG TO OFFER HIM ANOTHER OPTION.

SO-- HERE'S MY NEW PLAN.

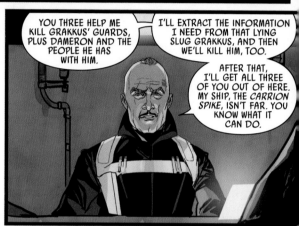

YOU THREE HELP ME KILL GRAKKUS' GUARDS, PLUS DAMERON AND THE PEOPLE HE HAS WITH HIM.

I'LL EXTRACT THE INFORMATION I NEED FROM THAT LYING SLUG GRAKKUS, AND THEN WE'LL KILL HIM, TOO.

AFTER THAT, I'LL GET ALL THREE OF YOU OUT OF HERE. MY SHIP, THE CARRION SPIKE, ISN'T FAR. YOU KNOW WHAT IT CAN DO.

YOU ALL KNOW WHAT I CAN DO, TOO. NOT SUCH A BAD THING TO HAVE AGENT TEREX IN YOUR DEBT.

SO, MY FRIENDS. WHAT DO YOU SAY?

THNK

TIME TO KILL.

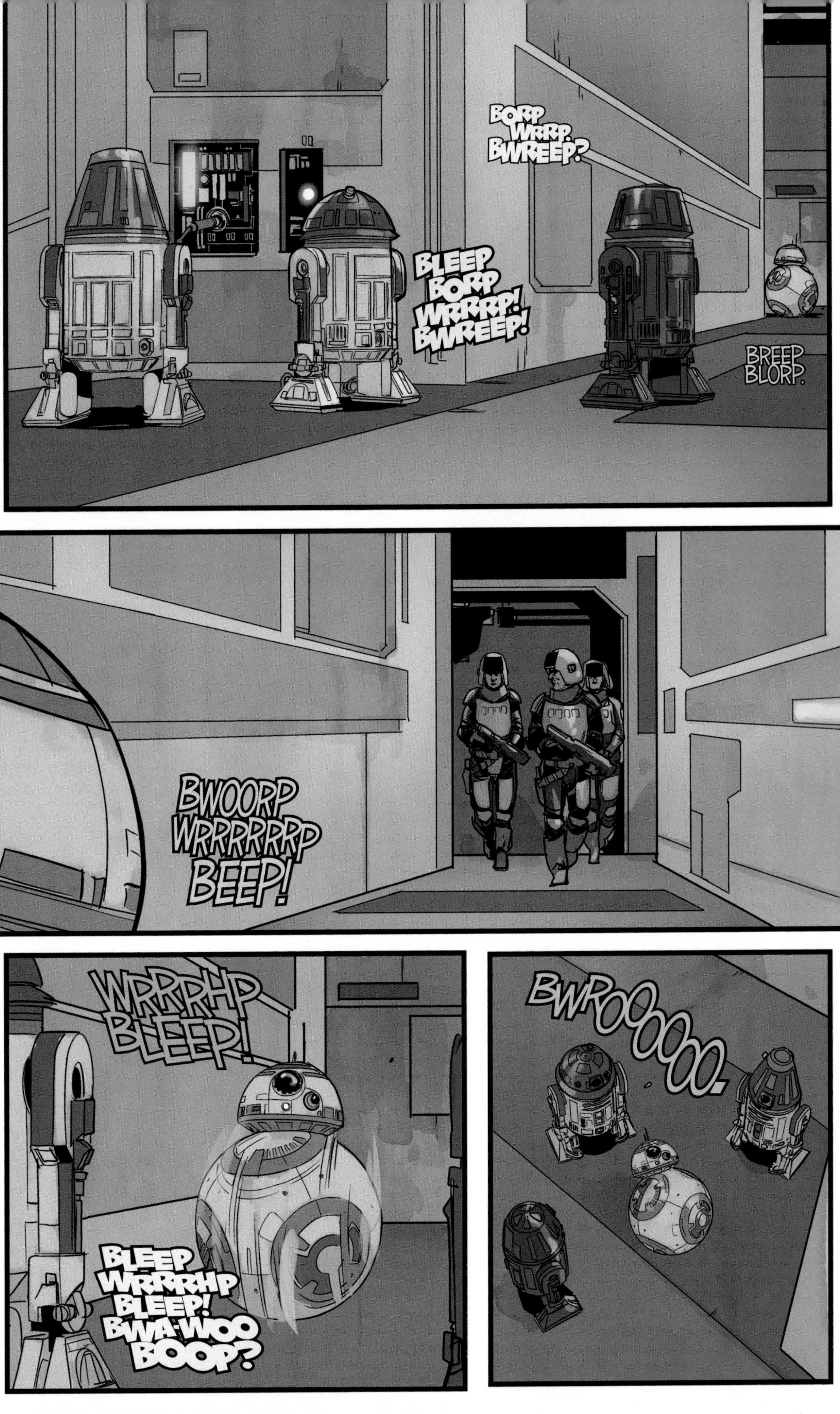
BORP WRRP. BWREEP?
BLEEP BORP WRRRP! BWREEP!
BREEP BLORP.
BWOORP WRRRRRRP BEEP!
WRRRHP BLEEP!
BLEEP WRRRHP BLEEP! BWA-WOO BOOP?
BWROOOOOO.

KIND OF QUIET DOWN IN THE PRISON RECENTLY, DON'T YOU THINK?

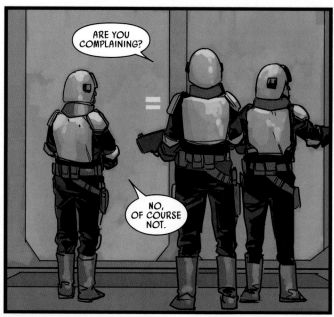

ARE YOU COMPLAINING?

NO, OF COURSE NOT.

IT'S JUST WHEN THINGS GET REALLY CALM... MAKES ME NERVOUS.

SSK!

THAT'S DUMB. IF IT'S CALM, IT JUST MEANS WE'RE DOING OUR JOBS.

WHAT ARE YOU AFRAID OF?

YOU NEVER KNOW.

SOMETIMES TROUBLE JUST FALLS OUT OF THE--

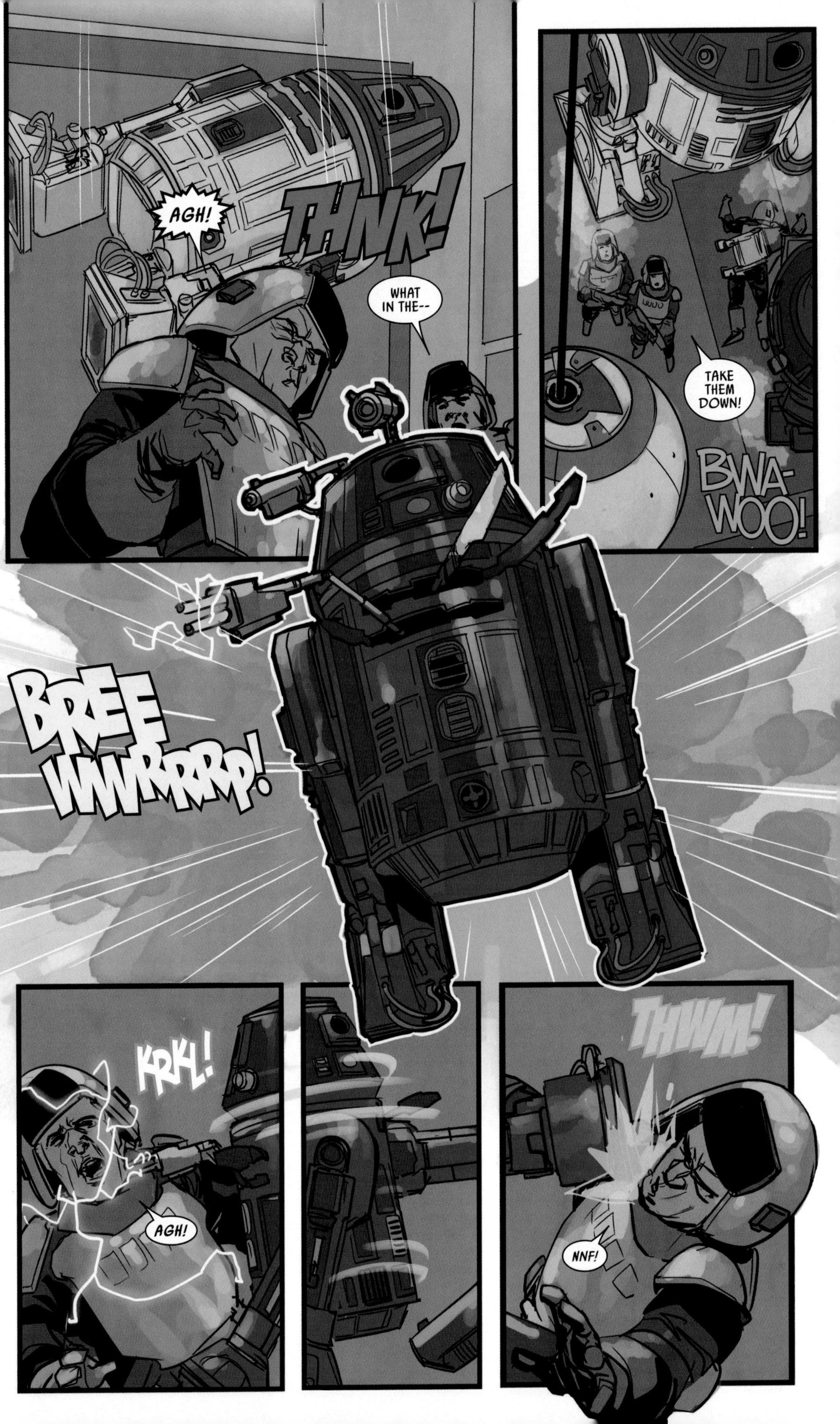
AGH!
THNK!
WHAT IN THE--
TAKE THEM DOWN!
BWA-WOO!
BREE WWRRRP!
KRKL!
AGH!
THWM!
NNF!

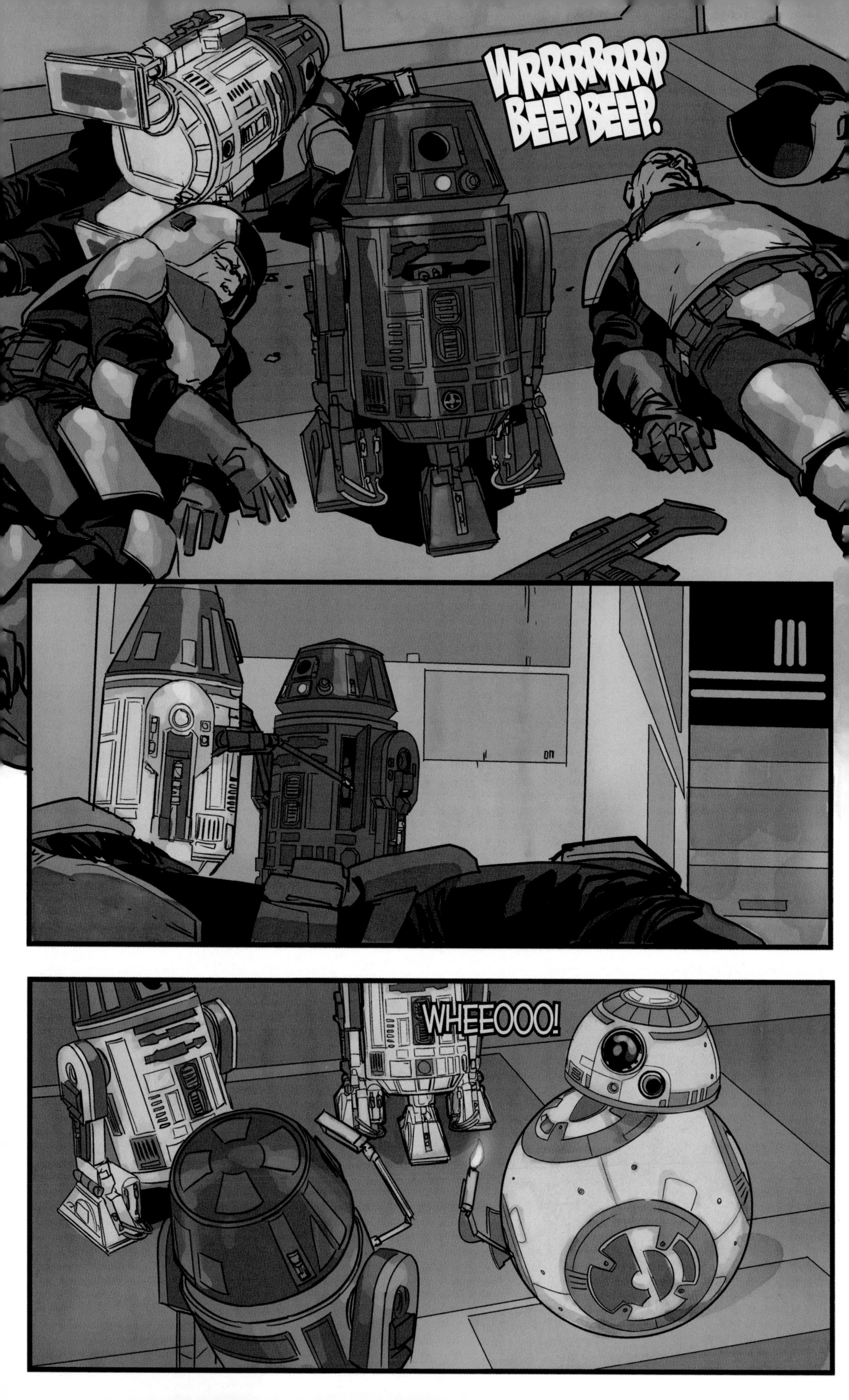
WRRRRRRP BEEP BEEP.
WHEEOOO!

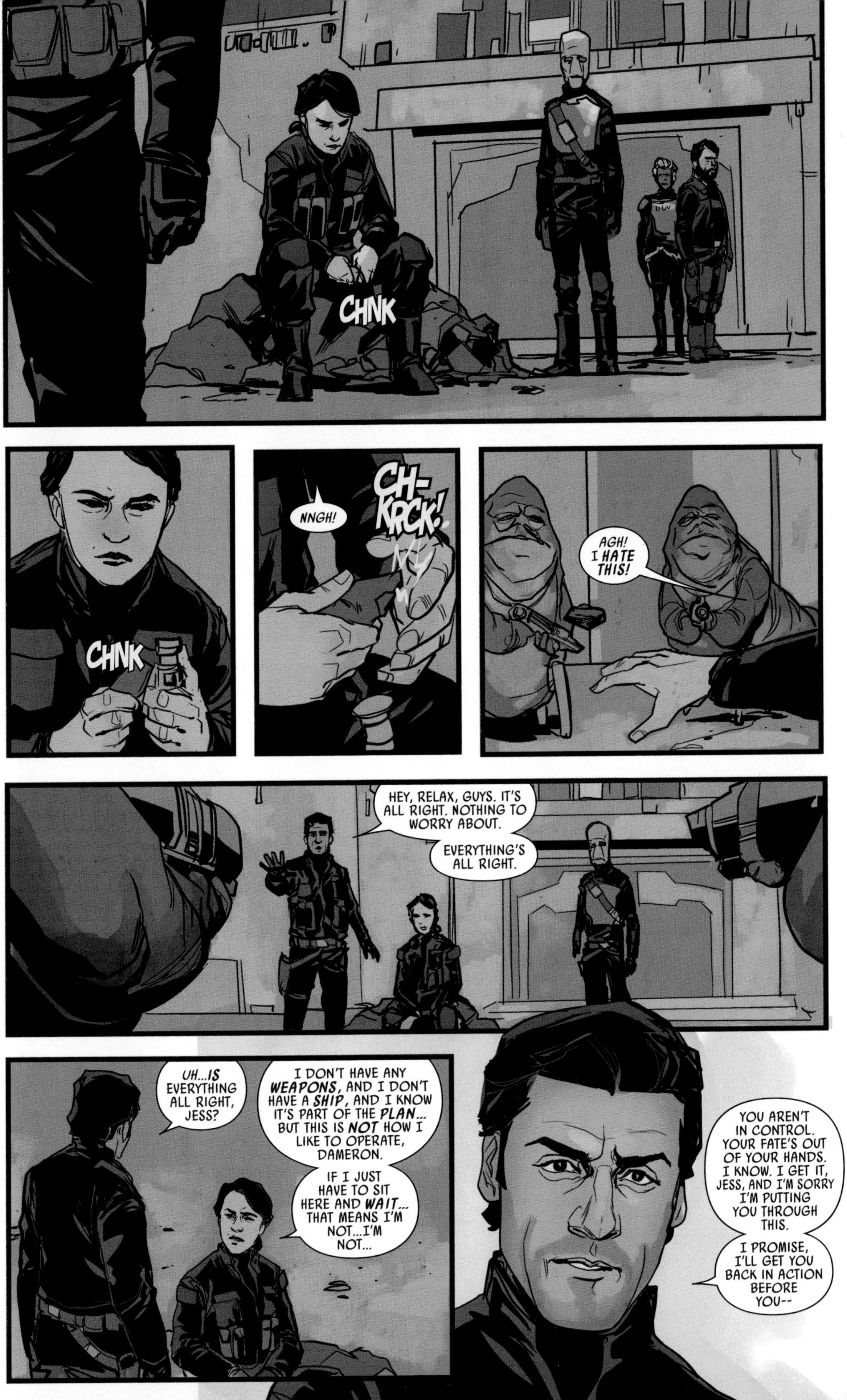
CHNK
CHNK
NNGH!
CH-KRCK!
AGH! I HATE THIS!
HEY, RELAX, GUYS. IT'S ALL RIGHT. NOTHING TO WORRY ABOUT.
EVERYTHING'S ALL RIGHT.
UH...IS EVERYTHING ALL RIGHT, JESS?
I DON'T HAVE ANY WEAPONS, AND I DON'T HAVE A SHIP, AND I KNOW IT'S PART OF THE PLAN... BUT THIS IS NOT HOW I LIKE TO OPERATE, DAMERON.
IF I JUST HAVE TO SIT HERE AND WAIT... THAT MEANS I'M NOT...I'M NOT...
YOU AREN'T IN CONTROL. YOUR FATE'S OUT OF YOUR HANDS. I KNOW. I GET IT, JESS, AND I'M SORRY I'M PUTTING YOU THROUGH THIS.
I PROMISE, I'LL GET YOU BACK IN ACTION BEFORE YOU--

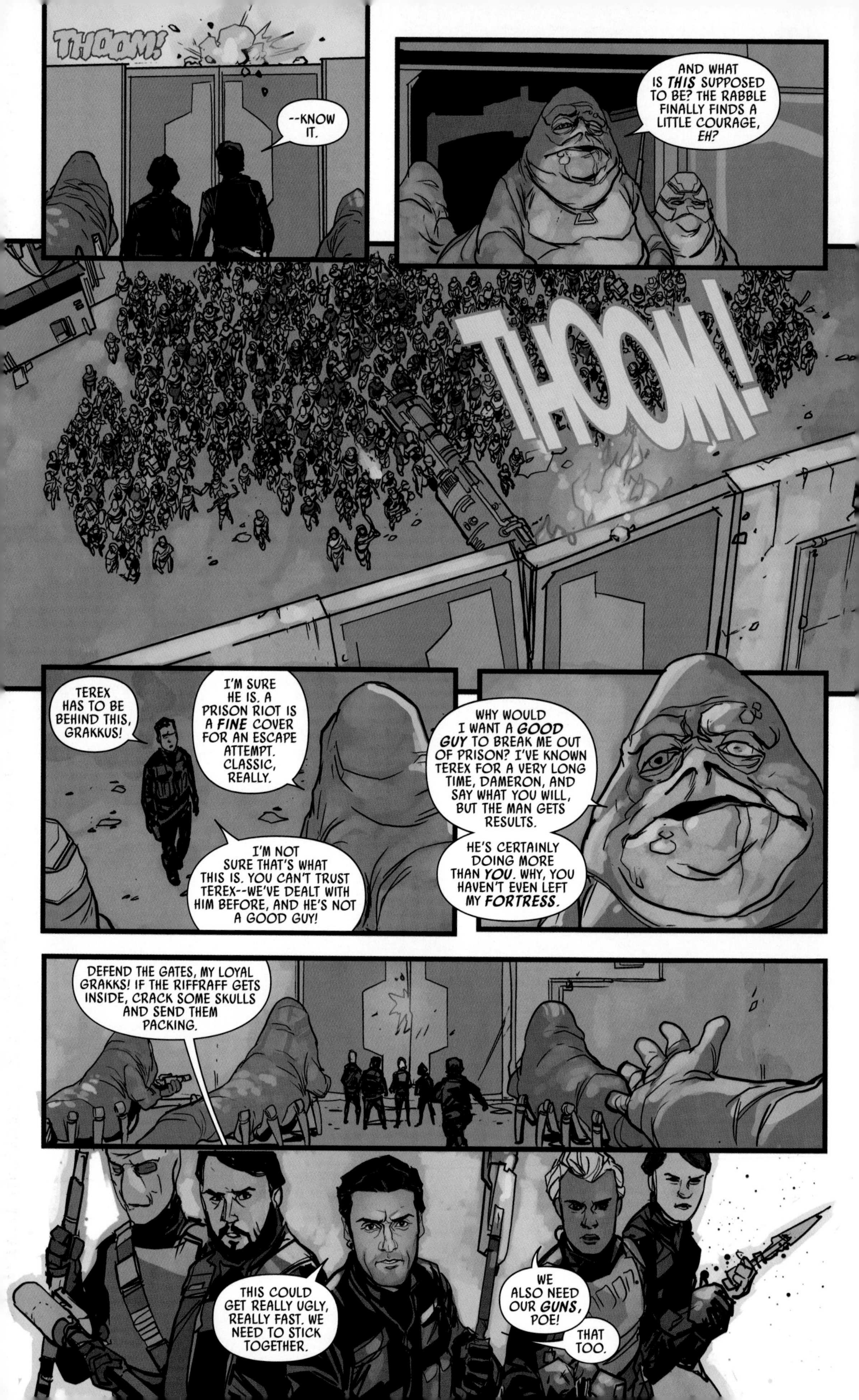
THOOM!
--KNOW IT.
AND WHAT IS THIS SUPPOSED TO BE? THE RABBLE FINALLY FINDS A LITTLE COURAGE, EH?
THOOM!
TEREX HAS TO BE BEHIND THIS, GRAKKUS!
I'M SURE HE IS. A PRISON RIOT IS A FINE COVER FOR AN ESCAPE ATTEMPT. CLASSIC, REALLY.
I'M NOT SURE THAT'S WHAT THIS IS. YOU CAN'T TRUST TEREX--WE'VE DEALT WITH HIM BEFORE, AND HE'S NOT A GOOD GUY!
WHY WOULD I WANT A GOOD GUY TO BREAK ME OUT OF PRISON? I'VE KNOWN TEREX FOR A VERY LONG TIME, DAMERON, AND SAY WHAT YOU WILL, BUT THE MAN GETS RESULTS.
HE'S CERTAINLY DOING MORE THAN YOU. WHY, YOU HAVEN'T EVEN LEFT MY FORTRESS.
DEFEND THE GATES, MY LOYAL GRAKKS! IF THE RIFFRAFF GETS INSIDE, CRACK SOME SKULLS AND SEND THEM PACKING.
THIS COULD GET REALLY UGLY, REALLY FAST. WE NEED TO STICK TOGETHER.
WE ALSO NEED OUR GUNS, POE!
THAT TOO.

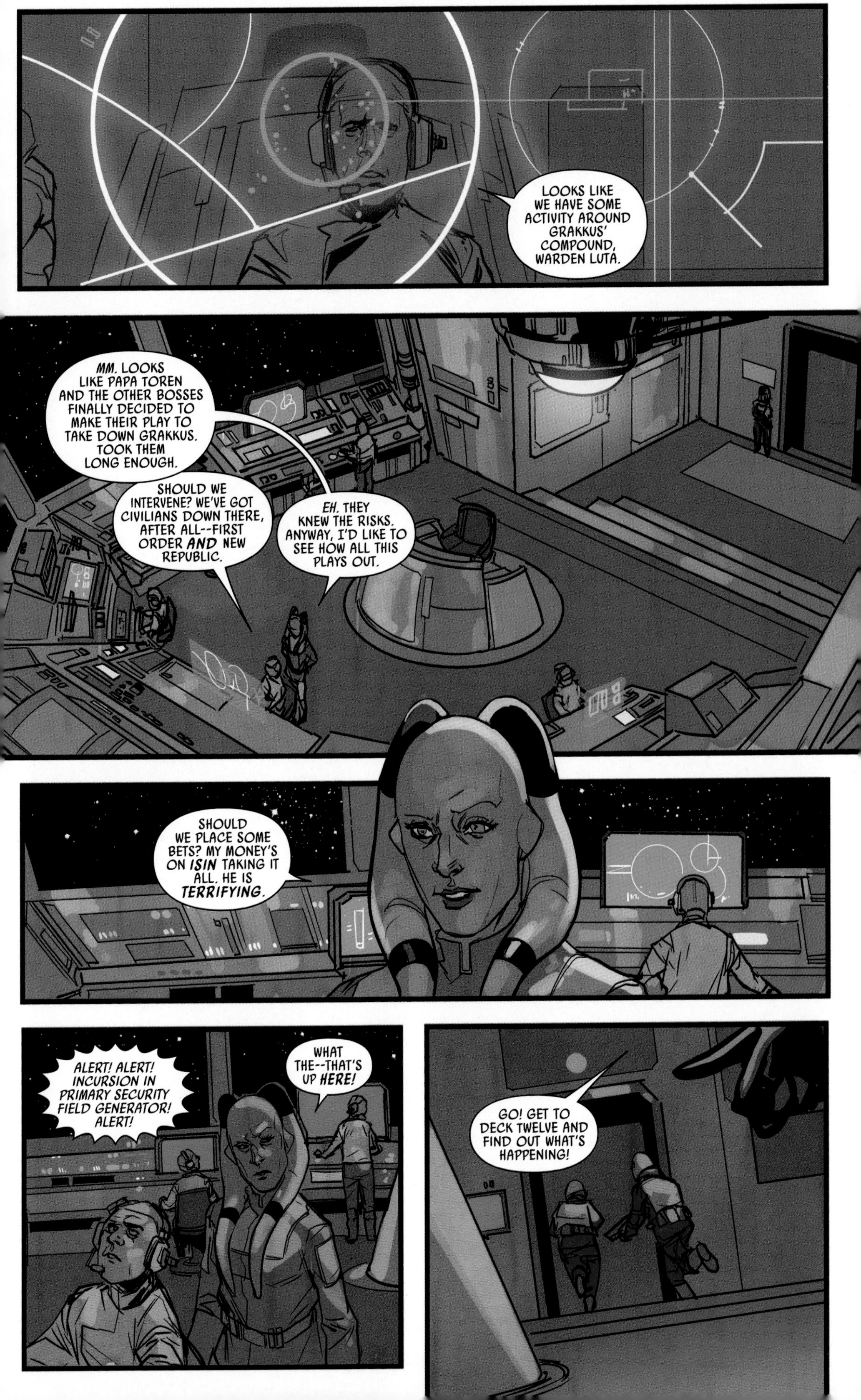
LOOKS LIKE WE HAVE SOME ACTIVITY AROUND GRAKKUS' COMPOUND, WARDEN LUTA.
MM. LOOKS LIKE PAPA TOREN AND THE OTHER BOSSES FINALLY DECIDED TO MAKE THEIR PLAY TO TAKE DOWN GRAKKUS. TOOK THEM LONG ENOUGH.
SHOULD WE INTERVENE? WE'VE GOT CIVILIANS DOWN THERE, AFTER ALL--FIRST ORDER AND NEW REPUBLIC.
EH. THEY KNEW THE RISKS. ANYWAY, I'D LIKE TO SEE HOW ALL THIS PLAYS OUT.
SHOULD WE PLACE SOME BETS? MY MONEY'S ON ISIN TAKING IT ALL. HE IS TERRIFYING.
ALERT! ALERT! INCURSION IN PRIMARY SECURITY FIELD GENERATOR! ALERT!
WHAT THE--THAT'S UP HERE!
GO! GET TO DECK TWELVE AND FIND OUT WHAT'S HAPPENING!

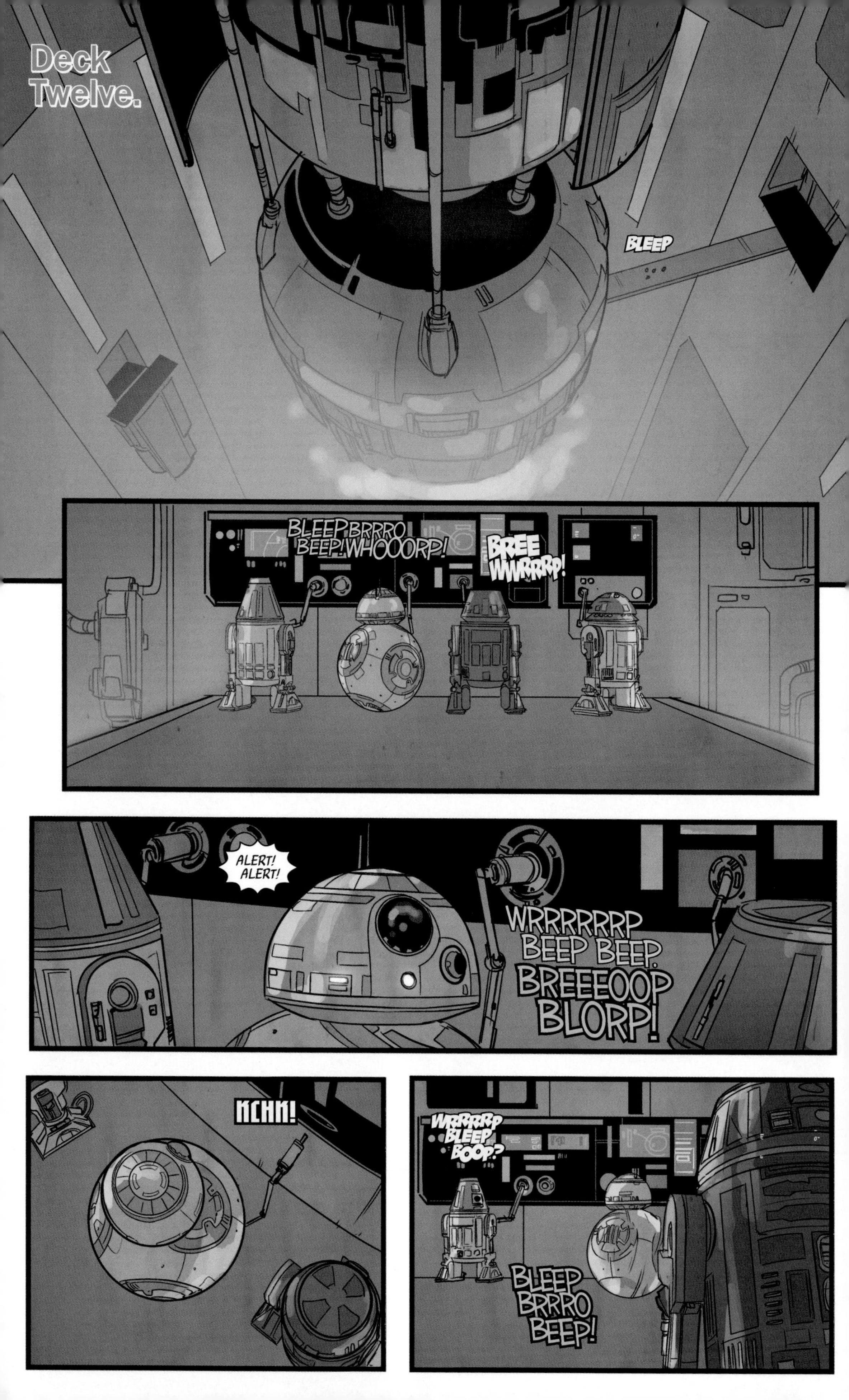
Deck Twelve.
BLEEP
BLEEP BRRRO BEEP! WHOOORP!
BREE WWRRRP!
ALERT! ALERT!
WRRRRRRP BEEP BEEP. BREEEOOP BLORP!
KCHH!
WRRRRP BLEEP BOOP?
BLEEP BRRRO BEEP!

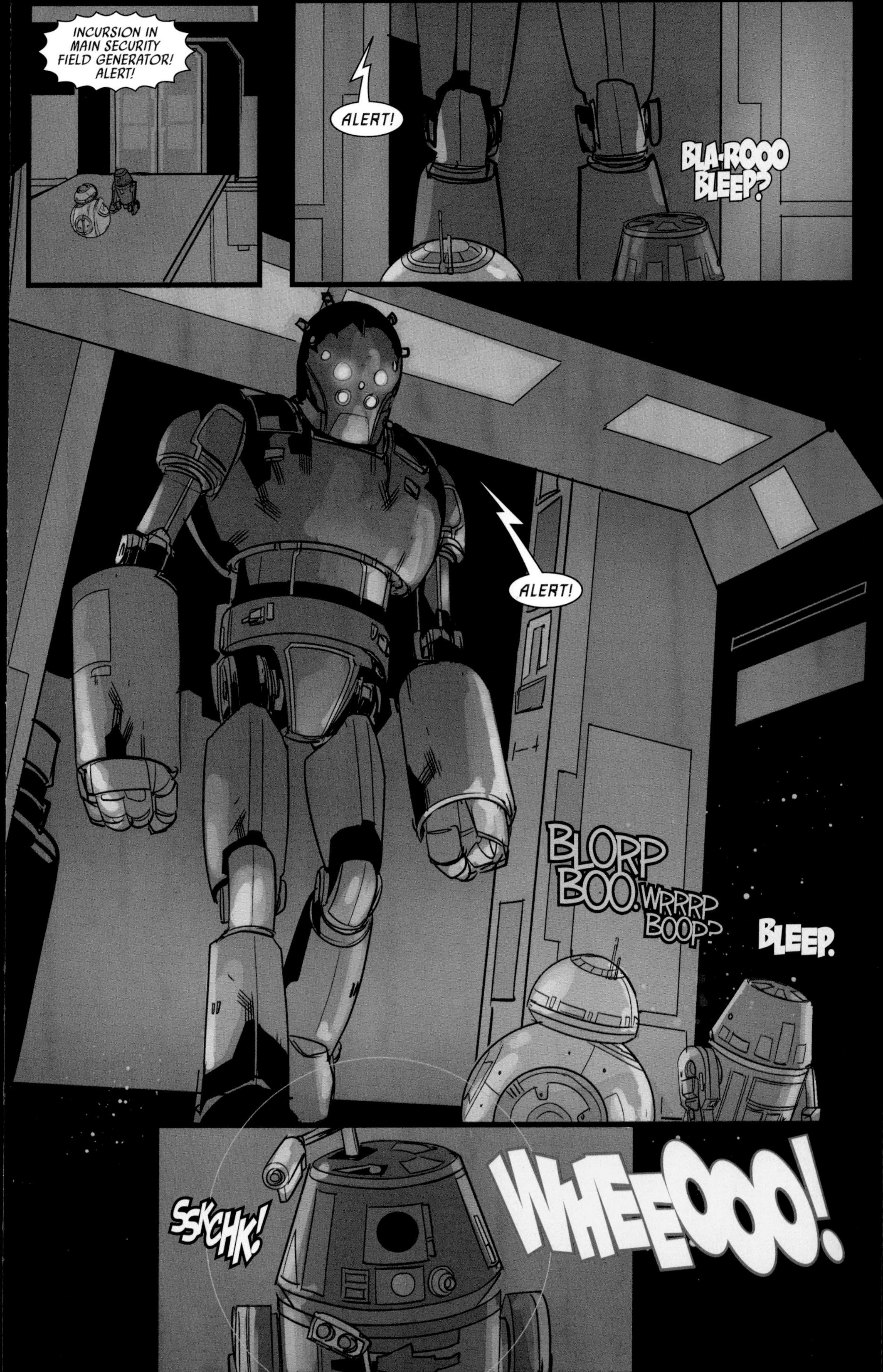
INCURSION IN MAIN SECURITY FIELD GENERATOR! ALERT!
ALERT!
BLA-ROOO BLEEP?
ALERT!
BLORP BOO.
WRRRP BOOP?
BLEEP.
SSKCHK!
WHEEOOO!

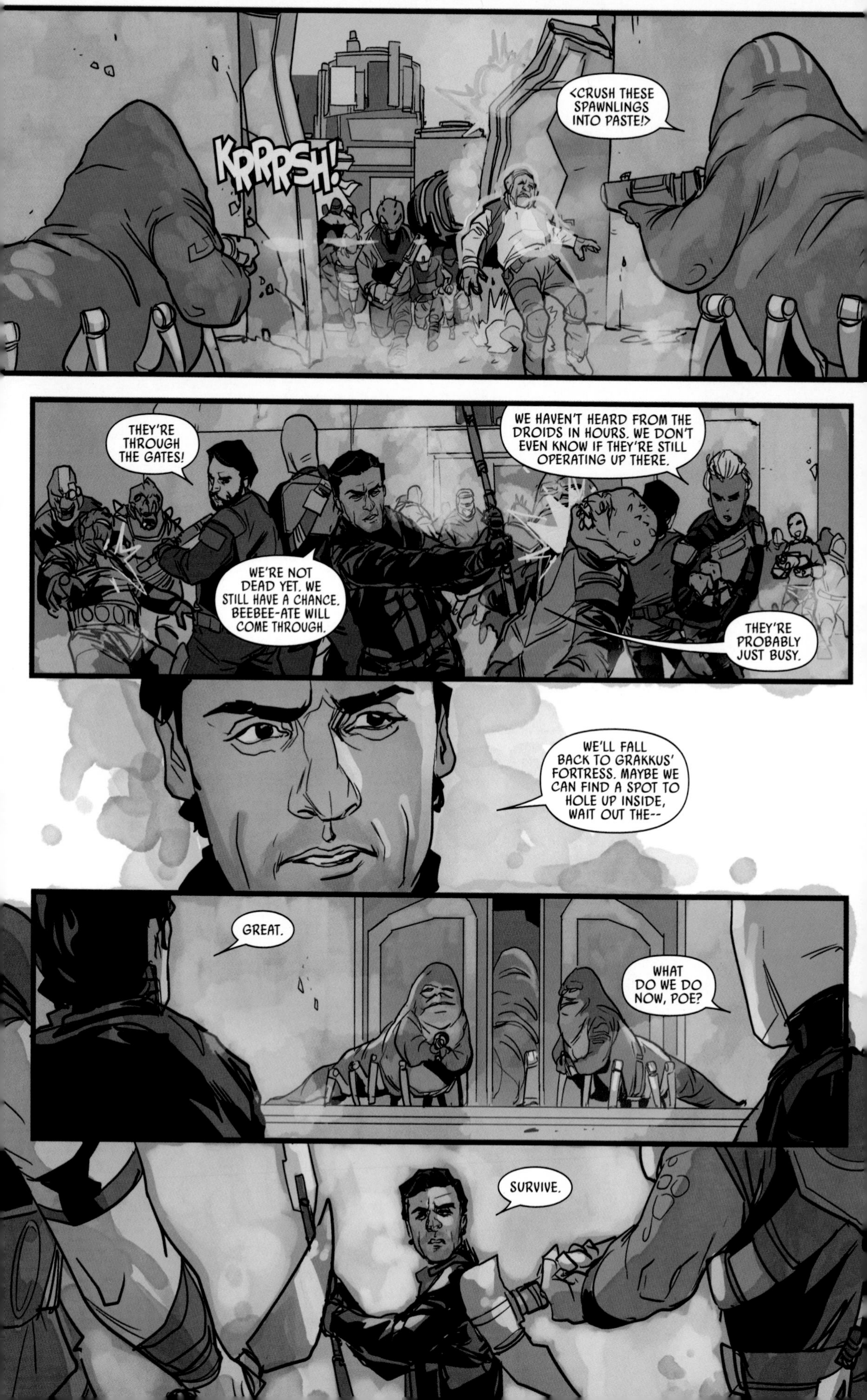
<CRUSH THESE SPAWNLINGS INTO PASTE!>
KRRRSH!
THEY'RE THROUGH THE GATES!
WE HAVEN'T HEARD FROM THE DROIDS IN HOURS. WE DON'T EVEN KNOW IF THEY'RE STILL OPERATING UP THERE.
WE'RE NOT DEAD YET. WE STILL HAVE A CHANCE. BEEBEE-ATE WILL COME THROUGH.
THEY'RE PROBABLY JUST BUSY.
WE'LL FALL BACK TO GRAKKUS' FORTRESS. MAYBE WE CAN FIND A SPOT TO HOLE UP INSIDE, WAIT OUT THE--
GREAT.
WHAT DO WE DO NOW, POE?
SURVIVE.

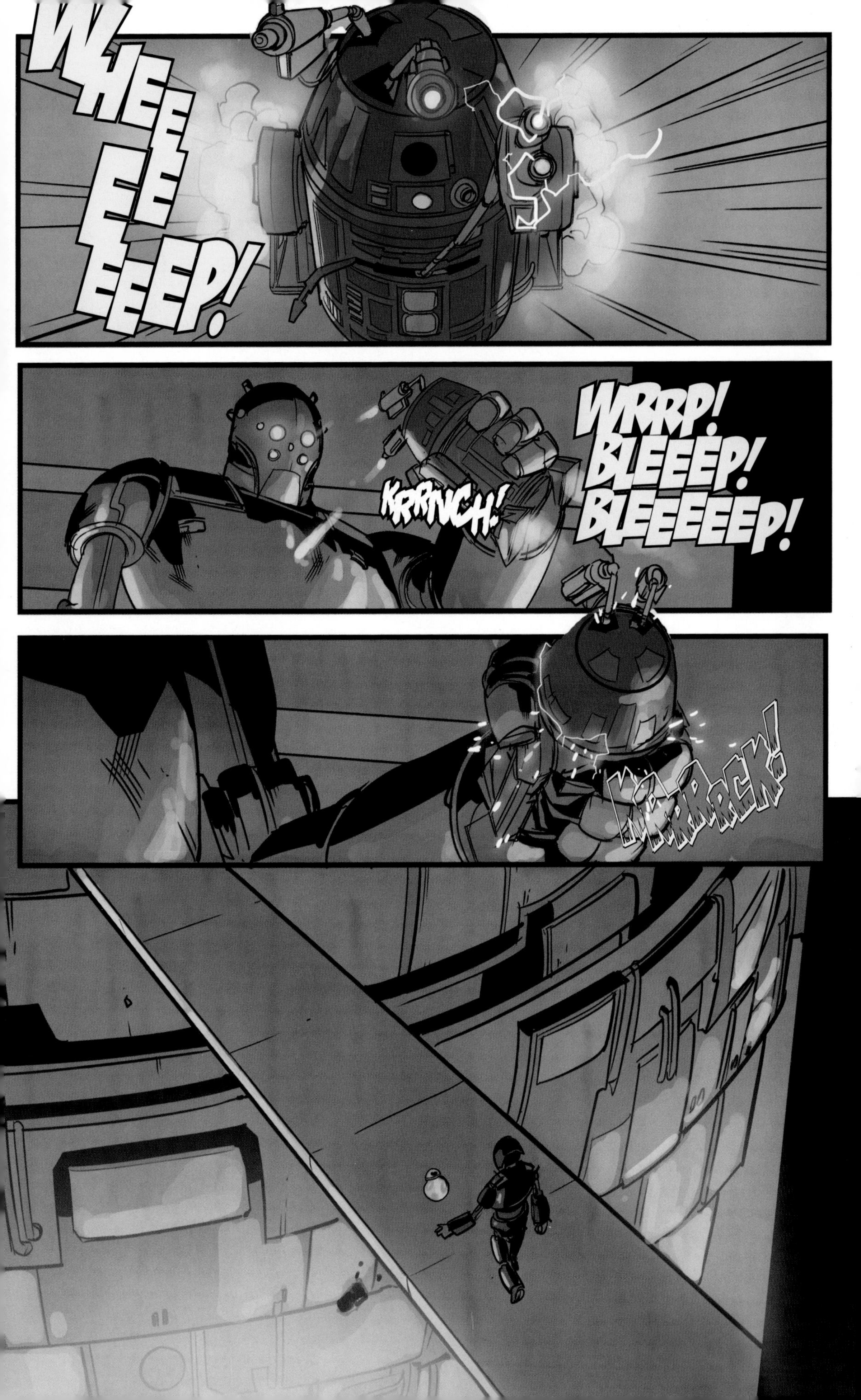
WHEEEEEEEEP!
KRRNCH!
WRRP! BLEEEP! BLEEEEEP!
KRRRCK!

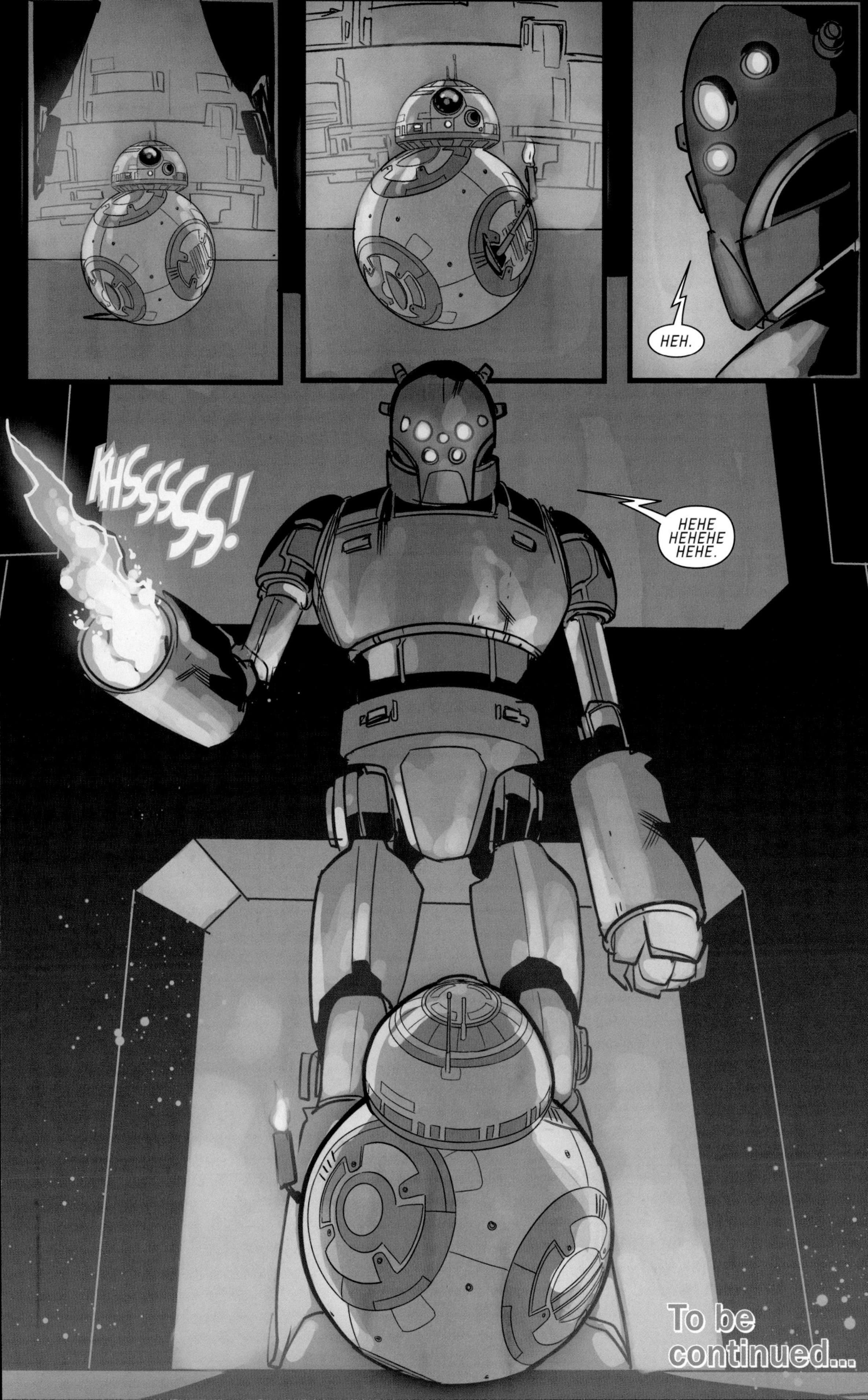
HEH.
KHSSSSSS!
HEHE HEHEHE HEHE.
To be continued...

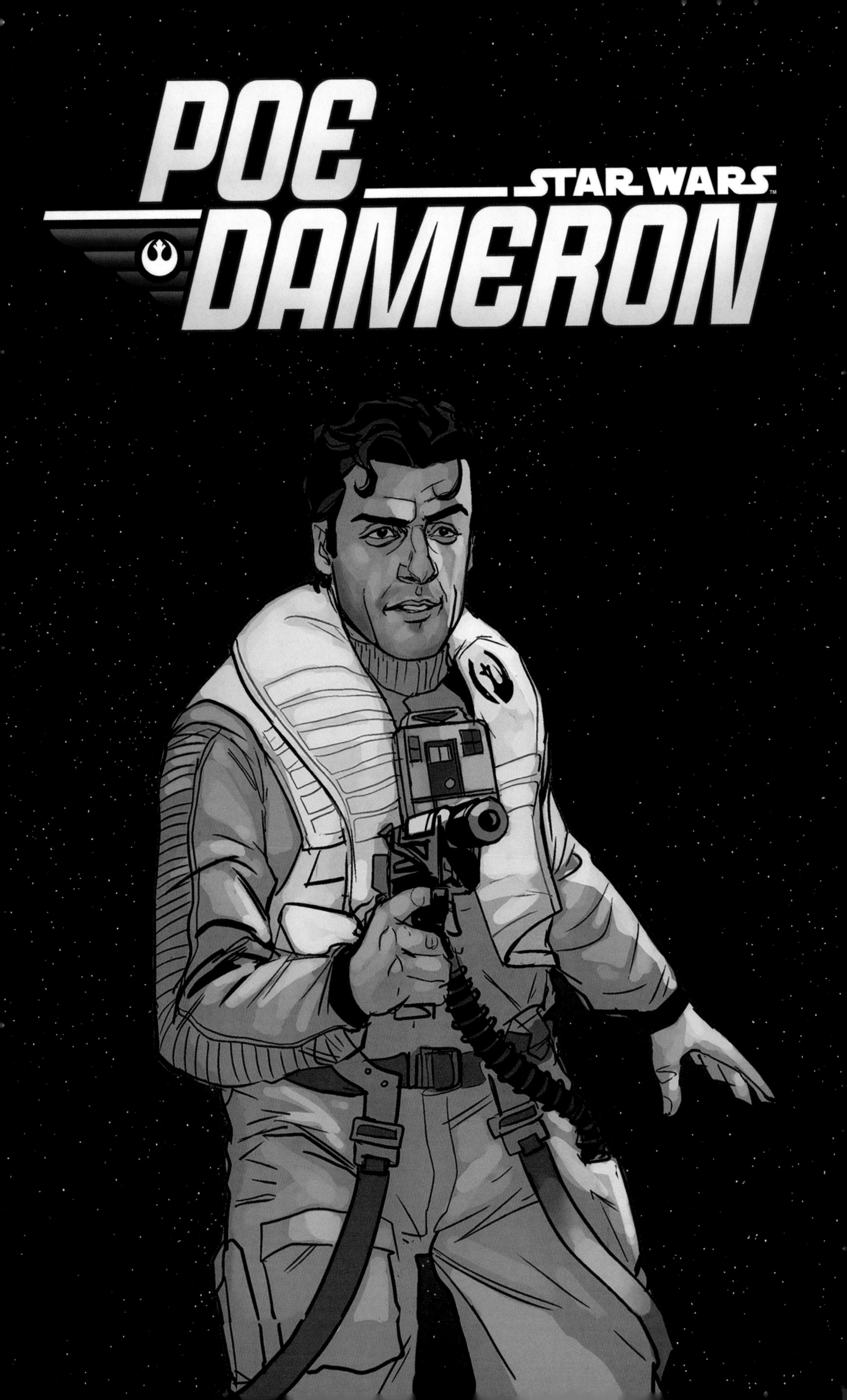
POE
STAR WARS
DAMERON

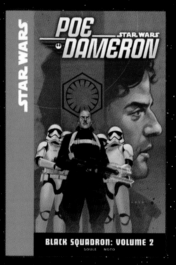
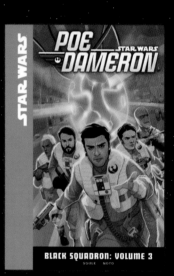
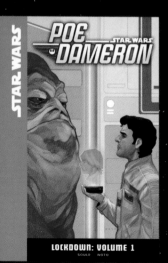
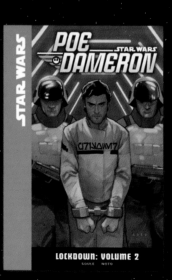
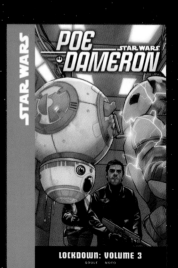